Monica

Monica is a sweet, happy, buck-toothed, teenage girl. When she was younger, she was known for being intolerant of disrespect and always stood up for her friends. That is, unless Jimmy-Five and Smudge would cause her trouble, then Monica would bash them with her favorite plush blue bunny, Samson! Still, occasionally, she does her classic bunny bashings as a teen, but has chilled out when it comes to Jimmy-Five, who has been catching her attention a lot more lately. Monica is the leader of the gang because of her honest and charismatic—and powerful—personality.

J-Five

Jimmy-Five, or J-Five, has always been picked on for his speech impediment. He used to lisp, which caused him to switch letters around, such as r's for w's, when he would speak. He has grown out of that as a teen, unless he's nervous, which typically happens around a certain girl. He also was picked on because of the five strands of hair he had on his head, which have all sort of filled out as a teen. Still, J-Five is sometimes made fun of for his hair, but he doesn't let it get to him as much anymore! When J-Five was young, he would often try to steal Monica's blue bunny from her and attempt to take over as leader of the gang with his questionable schemes. J-Five is no longer focused on being head of the gang as much as he's focused on being close with his friends, and closer to one friend in particular...

Smudge

Smudge has never liked water and prefers his messy and dirty lifestyle over showers, rain, swimming, or even drinking water any day, but he's warmed up to taking showers as a teen... sort of. He cleans up sometimes mainly because the opinion of girls has started to matter to him, unlike when he was a kid. Smudge loves sports, especially skateboarding and soccer because of how radical they are. He also loves comics, and shares this love with his best friend, J-Five! Smudge is kind of the "handyman" of the gang, always helping his friends in times of need but typically also messing everything up.

Maggy

Maggy is Monica's best friend, always having her back and being there for her in good times and bad. Maggy is also a huge lover of cats. Maggy has always had a voracious appetite, mostly eating watermelons but never discriminating against any other food put in front of her. Maggy is more conscious of what she eats now... perhaps a little too much. She is virtually obsessed with proper nutrition, sports, and exercise instead of eating anything she sees.

#1 "Who Can Afford the Price of Friendship Today?!"

Characters, Story, and Illustration created by Mauricio de Sousa
DENNIS OYAFUSO, DIOGO NASCIMENTO—Cover Artists
MAURICIO DE SOUSA, MARINA TAKEDA E SOUSA, FLÁVIO TEIXEIRA DE JESUS—Script
JOSÉ APARECIDO CAVALCANTE, LINO PAES, ROBERTO M. PEREIRA—Pencils
MAURO SOUZA, ZAZO AGUILAR—Illustrations
CRISTINA H. ANDO, JAIME PODAVIN, TATIANA M. SANTOS, VIVIANE YAMABUCHI—Inks
CARLOS KINA—Lettering
A. MAURICIO SOUSA NETO, ANTÔNIO R. F. GUEDES, KAIO RENATO BRUDER—Finishes
JAE HYUNG WOO, MARCELO KINA, MARIA JÚLIA S. BELLUCCI—Colorists
MARIA DE FÁTIMA A. CLARO—Art Coordination
SANDRO ANTONIO DA SILVA—Script Supervisor
ALICE K. TAKEDA—Executive Director
SIDNEY GUSMAN—Editorial Planner
ÍVANA MELLO—Original editor
PECCAVI TRANSLATIONS—Original Translations

Special thanks to LOURDES GALIANO, RODRIGO PAIVA, MÔNICA SOUSA, and MAURICO DE SOUSA

© 2019 Mauricio de Sousa Editora – All Rights reserved.
Originally published as Monica Teen #3 by Panini Comics. ©MSP- Brasil/2012

www.turmadamonica.com.br
All other editorial material ©2019 by Charmz.
All rights reserved.

JEFF WHITMAN—Editor, Production
KARR ANTUNES—Editorial Intern
JIM SALICRUP
Editor-in-Chief

Charmz is an imprint of Papercutz.

PB ISBN: 978-1-5458-0218-2
HC ISBN: 978-1-5458-0219-9

Printed in China
January 2019

Charmz books may be purchased for business or promotional use.
For information on bulk purchases please contact Macmillan
Corporate and Premium Sales Department at
(800) 221-7945 x5442

Distributed by Macmillan
First Charmz Printing

6

9

PAUSE FOR THE FLASHBACK

MON! I'M GOING TO GET AN ICE CREAM! YOU WANT ONE?

ARE YOU SURE YOU'LL ONLY HAVE ONE, MAGGY?

YES! I NEED TO MAINTAIN MY SILHOUETTE, GIRL!

MY OVER-EATER DAYS ARE IN THE PAST!

14

19

CHAPTER 2 - SATURDAY

BROTHERS

BROTHERS

mandonna

I JUST WOKE UP, MAGGY! I'LL SEE YOU IN A LITTLE BIT OVER AT J'S--

Gossip

HEY! DO YOU THINK IF WE PUT ALL OUR MONEY TOGETHER WE COULD RENT A HOUSE OUT SOMEWHERE REAL NICE?

WHAT? YOU'LL DO NO SUCH THING!

DON'T YOU EVEN THINK ABOUT IT! NOT WITHOUT AN ADULT PRESENT! NO WAY!

24

25

27

34

36

43

45

49

56

57

59

64

74

91

93

99

106

109

111

MORE GRAPHIC NOVELS AVAILABLE FROM

**STITCHED #1
"THE FIRST DAY OF THE
REST OF HER LIFE"**

**STITCHED #2
"LOVE IN THE TIME
OF ASSUMPTION"**

**G.F.F.s #1
"MY HEART LIES
IN THE 90s"**

**G.F.F.s #2
"WITCHES GET
THINGS DONE"**

**CHLOE #1
"THE NEW GIRL"**

**CHLOE #2 "THE QUEEN
OF HIGH SCHOOL"**

**CHLOE #3
"FRENEMIES"**

**CHLOE #4
"RAINY DAY"**

**SCARLET ROSE #1
"I KNEW I'D MEET YOU"**

**SCARLET ROSE #2
"I'LL GO WHERE YOU GO"**

**SCARLET ROSE #3
"I THINK I LOVE YOU"**

**SCARLET ROSE #4
"YOU WILL ALWAYS BE MINE"**

**AMY'S DIARY #1
"SPACE ALIEN...
ALMOST?"**

**SWEETIES #1
"CHERRY SKYE"**

MONICA ADVENTURES #1

**ANA AND THE
COSMIC RACE #1
"THE RACE BEGINS"**

Charmz graphic novels are available for $9.99 in paperback, and $14.99 in hardcover. Monica Adventures is available for $8.99 in paperback, and $13.99 in hardcover. Available from booksellers everywhere.

You can also order online from www.papercutz.com. Or call 1-800-886-1223, Monday through Friday, 9–5 EST. MC, Visa, and AmEx accepted. To order by mail, please add $5.00 for postage and handling for first book ordered, $1.00 for each additional book and make check payable to NBM Publishing.
Send to: Charmz, 160 Broadway, Suite 700, East Wing, New York, NY 10038.
Charmz graphic novels are also available wherever e-books are sold.

Charmz chat

Welcome to the exciting Charmz debut of MONICA ADVENTURES, brought to you by the Papercutz imprint devoted to romantic and fun graphic novels. We're incredibly excited to bring MONICA to you and to a whole new generation of North American fans. MONICA is created by the legendary cartoonist Mauricio de Sousa, a beloved comics maker with millions of fans worldwide.

MONICA originates from Brazil, where Monica, J-Five, Maggy, Smudge and Two To—Tony, (just Tony now) are all comicbook superstars. Known almost everywhere else in the world, Monica (and the gang) has been translated into many languages, has been celebrated in the international comics community and has won the coveted Yellow Kid award. MONICA is also credited with fostering friendship and understanding and for teaching generations of Brazilians how to read. Monica has starred in countless films, animated series, video games, shorts, books, stage shows, and countless adaptations. she is the Queen of Brazilian comics and even the cultural ambassador of Brazil for UNICEF.

Monica's first appearance in Jimmy Five's newspaper strip on March 3rd, 1963.
Even if you don't speak Portuguese, you can see the start of this comic rivalry!

Monica and friends have been together in comics for a long time—over 50 years, in fact. Cartoonist Mauricio de Sousa was inspired to create the cartoon Monica by his then-young daughter the real-life Monica, a stubborn little girl with a temper and a plush rabbit. He introduced her in the pages of his comic strip (pictured above) and she quickly became incredibly popular—with fans demanding to see more of this exciting and lovable character. Her series of comicbooks have been continuously published now for over 50 years, and millions of her comics are sold every month in Brazil. MONICA is a true, bonafide phenomenon.

The young Monica and her friends continue to star in their own comic, but a teenage Monica has a series of her own, as well. It's that series, called MONICA TEEN, that we're currently presenting here as this Charmz graphic novel series. Within these stories, you'll get a peek at the younger Monica and her friends in the flashback sequences. We'd love to publish the younger MONICA comics as a Papercutz graphic novel series…what do you think?

A SPECIAL MESSAGE FROM
MAURICIO DE SOUSA
THE CREATOR OF MONICA

There is a game that is played in almost every single comicbook production studio: adding "Easter eggs" and cameos to the books that are based on personalities of friends, colleagues, the boss, the directors, etc. Much like the way Alfred Hitchcock used to appear in his own movies. Or more recently, much like Stan Lee has been appearing in the latest Marvel super hero movies. In "Who Can Afford the Price of Friendship Today?", written by Flavio Teixeira, there are some examples of this game that serve as homages to his friends, colleagues, and so on. For the other individuals in the studio, this serves as a sort of improvised *Where's Waldo?* game, trying to find which of themselves or common friend of theirs made an appearance.

To the audience, sometimes, these small special appearances go completely unnoticed, so I am discussing this here so that I can help you enjoy a custom that we have at the studio; something to look out for and enjoy in future editions of MONICA ADVENTURES.

Just for you to get a clearer picture, in this edition the homages went to Osamu Tezuka (master of Manga, creator of Astro Boy), Kevin Smith (comics and cinema writer/director, comics store owner), Dik Browne (*Hägar the Horrible*), Paulo Back (another MONICA writer), Roberto M. Pereira (who sometimes likes to self-homage himself since he is the story's illustrator), Flavio Teixeira (the writer of this story), Rene Goscinny and Albert Uderzo (*Asterix*), Will Eisner (*The Spirit*), Sidney Gusman (Mauricio de Sousa Productions's editorial planner – in the story he was the owner of the comicbook shop), Silvia Back (Paulo's wife) and her many cats, George Lucas (*Star Wars*), and every once in a while another person peppered into different places in the story.

Editor Jeff Whitman (right), a Monica fanatic for years, had the pleasure of visiting Mauricio in his amazing studio in Brazil.

Photo credit: The *actual, real-life* **Monica**!

Some folks might feel inclined to believe that this exercise doesn't go with the "style" or "flow" of the story... I, however, am of a different opinion. I believe that these innocent and good-natured additions by the creators of the story only work to enrich the reality of our stories. In many ways, this serves as a tool to make the narration flow and the story more colorful and interesting. By adding different human voices and emotions we find ways to make the stories more attractive to our fans. So, with care and in the right way, we continue to do and allow these "games." In the future, I hope to tell you more details of how and why things happen in our stories and in real life... in the script and the lives of the creators.

Mauricio

Mauricio de Sousa

Be sure to pick up MONICA ADVENTURES #2 "We Fought Each Other as Kids... Now We're in Love?!" available now wherever books are sold. Will Monica and J-Five finally have their chance together? Don't miss MONICA ADVENTURES #2!

Want even more MONICA? Interested in seeing her and her friends's classic adventures? Well, write in and let us know!

STAY IN TOUCH!

EMAIL: whitman@papercutz.com
WEB: Papercutz.com
TWITTER: @papercutzgn
INSTAGRAM: @papercutzgn
FACEBOOK: PAPERCUTZGRAPHICNOVELS
FANMAIL: Charmz, 160 Broadway, Suite 700, East Wing, New York, NY 10038

31901064280490